To Kayley, for your inspiration:
I looked at you one day and asked,
"Did I ever say I love you?" and your
reply was, "Yes, Daddy, you say that
everyday."

D.K.C.

To my dad
Who always encouraged
my scribblings.

T.V.W

Library of Congress Control Number 2007902857
ISBN 978-1-4243-3918-1

10 To 2 Children's Books is dedicated to helping others.
A portion of our profits is donated to charity.

Written by Daryl K. Cobb
Illustrated by Traci Van Wagoner

www.10to2childrensbooks.com

Printed in China
First Printing 2007

Daddy Did I Ever Say?

I Love You, Love You, Every Day

To: Isabella
Enjoy reading this
with your Daddy.

Written by
Daryl K. Cobb

Illustrated by
Traci Van Wagoner

10 To 2 Children's Books / Clinton

I love you
when you squeeze me tight.
I love you
when you say good night.

I love it when you tickle me
and mom says stop
it is time to sleep.

I feel so safe
when you're around.
You pick me up
when I fall down.

But that's okay,
I am TOUGH!

I love you,
don't stay mad too long.
I cry a tear,
the anger's gone.

Wrapped around
my little thumb,
Mommy says.
I say that's dumb.

Sometimes
my days are just too long.
You hold me
till my tears are gone.

You kiss me once
upon my head,
then tuck me tightly
into bed.